sky so wide, i could find you
anywhere

MIDWESTERN INFINITY DOCTRINE

ULRICH JESSE K. BAER

Midwestern Infinity Doctrine

ISBN-13: 978-1-954899-11-7
ISBN-10: 1-954899-11-4

Cover design by Mike Corrao

www.apocalypse-party.com

Printed in the U.S.A

I wrote this while I was crawling out of hell
Still radioactive & smoking still
Verymuch alive

CONTENTS

Prologue:
Time Forgeries

We arrive at the kiln without a thought/ evacuated for our progenitors—the opening mouthed dark confronts them

Torrentially, flames lick through my body, my jacket goes jagging as they tear through. No escape from the ethereal fire—the body is ballasting in the night, autumn polished its wound dawning figureheads. And I rupture the seams my corporeal being starts to as vessels harden, the glaze sets. Different streaks alter themselves bifurcating with the held light, I am worn out to branches. I'll sleep in the empty quilt and forget that stirring pinetrees tussled. The new jersey slopes ate my body—I become a tone. A vibrating-up on a haunted string by a better note, forgotten.

That Your eyes glitter with lurking malice, green ridges shaded the tree lines breaking into your most secret desire. A chemical symbol combusts when I pick another reading you strip a world into its womb. But I huddle with Jesus in the mountainhollow, and start the exegesis, some nativity scenes we consecrate when the fire is a ravaging of a space, the vacuum seals. Quietude walks the land hollow. Until I arrive at a desert I remember you in. There's not enough shade in this world, but He's screaming to shove the tinder through the mouth, faster, slower now to temper-pace.

We have argued all the evenings in the car and I drawstring tie my hood in, close the breach. Space ushers us towards the new, bizarre forms, finagled with the shedding light. I drip glaze allover. It sucks me up.

Keep your neon glowing back at me. Stoke it with tinder, hands aren't delicate enough for this world.

I am learning that what you went to do with me is to need some body else? I am leaning into this learning, slower curves redress. Do you remember why we came here? Because you kneaded this You tooled it through yourself, evocable grandeur when decaying, leaves are a crown, yr remote, I'm god's eyes. I can't remember what we were fighting about but later you'll promise me an endlessness where I'll consume all the flesh I'm too afraid from a cold in my body to eat now: fetid figures slink. Anyplace else.

Is this enough glitter for a set piece? Show images to animals, to slake the desideratum of an animus we left behind, while gd's dreaming he plays with us.

A bad hand deer, make artifice. You don't wake. Me from the lostworld, intervals irresolute as a lyre string plucked taut, to curve the world into its purls. Water cuts it reiterates.

The difference between living and dying is fuzzy logic. So animate the cellular automata to me and purge, we'll build anew one. In the mimesis of the old one I harbored, it stings. Glassy disks, the moon's crevice gets eaten out of place the fossa in the last verse, is theosis, play it at rest. All the sharp edges of your pottery, the body is wrought. From the looking like outliers we recur: self excessive data. Mangle your image is.

Eliding with the light. It's 4 AM in rural New Jersey Jessica Baer wake up how long have you been waiting. Here we are ourselves, when composed.

Gargantuan palm leaves unfurl the green before the asteroid falls. Back, in another dimension. Who animates your strings when your screamshouts shelled, and fallout, atomic matter sherds litter yr dressup. Pose for the big sink. The gulping promises grief, we are making a new utensil for you to ware ourselves down. Bitter philter, slaphappy rejoinder, losing sleep, sometimes a word's unsaid.

There is nothing emptier than this field in new jersey before the sun rises and guts it-again. Until we catch the light, fuming cane stalks. You were grafted with antimatter before you came, born again on this world. Strigillate yr surfaces unending, a vessel's indefinite to the sidelines.

Until the aliens come down, inventing rituals to summon them, our gravity for atomic graves you inverse, I slough aside, are you still rising?

Eidetic logic places you afterpastures, convulsed. Perform autoscopy at the limitrophes of the nothing that held you back. We revenge ourselves, on ourselves, glut. Will the wound swell, tumesce with ganglia. Weirding littler feelers, heads stage grace, say it later. Siren notes sighed the mellifluous undoes the ships, are you stalling. Really it's 2 PM in North Carolina and vines are knotting your feelings skinned. On earth we submerge, anagogic. I dance into a smaller cutout of myself in the car. Flick your cigarettes these fingers tear the thread weft-anything. Notches the self automating composition learns to read. A music box and the ballerina pirouette-escapes your vampyric gaze. Mine. To be holding patterns there is a counterfeit self, we lay it to waste.

In the future you live on a floating kiln barge and I stole this boat to gash inside the water. Towards You-foundered in my body, hulls by-itself.

Are you happy with the clay figures you've made.

II. Last Rites

Final New Jersey Transcript:

    [Scene: Exeunt its corners, the world does and we are trying]

    [Scene: New Jersey lawn chair where we were perched birds and clamored a way]

3.04 5:30

    I abandoned my daughter to the cat tails in the marsh. She has blue eyes have you found her, yet.

                          I was wearing a hood of softblue folds

5:31

No mother but I am still the searcher I am a search party after.

5:35

[Search lights beacon out, stunt themselves on mutating endless, angles draw up the lips of the givenfield.]

At night the sun is rising now we will coalesce at the diadem I wreathed you out of peonies, but who reads them anymore. Fingers tumble the loneliest shade is between them. Crease your fronds and press out the light.

6:00

I think I miss her.

III. It's Okay

He isn't mad at you, now.

MIDWESTERN INFINITY DOCTRINE

The Cosmic Dirge: Finale
Jessica Baer, Flash Gordon BY PROXY

"Do you want to know how it ends? It ends in your death, I have a violent vision of this on the highway, the midwest was the artery of"

A sinking disillusionment with tenses, time redistributes them. And I wake in a blank zone, cordoned from the fear some harvester.

When you die, and you will always, it is because I have traveled across galaxies to retrieve you but understand the necessary sacrifice whereby, through yr reunification with the godhead, gnoesis-poesis of the eternal mind, your hell will be sated, abated. But breath continues

voluting inbetween things, that togetherness-distance where we fix ourselves up with the looking after. I don't intervene; it's immaterial.

Space is haunted.

After yawning doors gasp shut,

I lock my spaceship in the cavity of a colossal unknown-vessel, the stars can't hold. I disembark myself kneed into the strange, to rush down lifeless hallways untouched by my mythology, until I arrive in the cosmic atrium where you are alive/undead because they have wired you up to the table, yr cosmic mind flashing above in a nebulous cloud. Hazing without: desire.

It takes nothing of me to let you die here, eaten by time/warps and solar flares. I have spent thousands of years navigating between constellations just to circumscribe this empty truth.

That you were never one.

One, Two, One, Two

So I'll just go back home now, keep driving the highways to work.

If you knew would you dissuade the future from ever arriving?

The Cosmic Muse Intervenes

A din when the train haunted its whistle

Inside your most secret dream, the wind parses. Don't disfigure yourself, wind

Just because you made a glowing mistake. All this supplication to make good, homing somewhere. Jessica Baer in the autumn of our flagging down the light took so long to reach you, because you were cold stone, mashed by the river its currentsdivine. Fragile architecture.

Cosmic Time

On Dreams
Transmission: High Frequency Blast
Coordinates: Andromeda Galaxy
Received—10:31
[radioslush]

*Ksssshhhhhhhhh*Every day I relearn that time is all affective investment; today I bilocated chronologically across the time-space locations of my life It always starts in new orleans where I was born at age 21 and then falling asleep in the back of Eliz's car as Zebulon drove us back against new england dark from a show in a deeplyhaunted Amherst basement Finally I am in Providence where I died Louis Bourgeois says nostalgia is mourning so to finish our conversation I don't think it's a necessary violence unless it's subverted into an ideological framework which is to say, let the past wash over you without holding it or expecting to

ksshhhhh

The worst thing is knowing that I can never go back Hunter to drinking wine as the sunsets through yr windows and you tell me about the vast collective conspiracy theory in the podcast where we can speak to the dead, if we try, and god is there do you think he can hear us

do you think he's mad at me

sshhhhksshhhhhh

33 Ways of Looking at Time Backwards an Anti-
timetime Lapse Video
Time Anti Time Time Doctrine

Here is what there was

So here is what I have so far in straining the possible/potential
articulations of timefulness & timelessness

Our Cosmic nothinghead

Time is in a sense only affective investment which serves as
the delineating force (cosmic law) between the bios and the
dead/undead of object-matter, where we live at this ledge of
spilling cascade-time and through our participation in thinky-
temporality, designate ourselves as social beings through parole
(our parole in the langue praxis). With recourse to special
relativity, affective time and quantitative (quantum) time
undergo the calculus of vacillation, speeding up or slowing down
relative to positionality (social and thus relative to massy bodies).

To situate ourselves within the polis is to situate our dreamful proximity to the idealism of linear time and it is in this sense that time becomes the privileged site where bare life is transformed into politicized life, reflexive with the coefficients of slowness and speed accounted for in a normativizing gesture towards homogenized time. Because my venus is in libra I propose this: that tonight love is the desire to transgress the bonds of the legislated self

At the commingling points of nostalgia grief and love, we rupture-time. If progress is as if a storm blown in from paradise that irrevocably hurls us into the "future," then love is the rupture that per versely conjoins the ideologically immobilized "past" with our present, where we touch grace.

We have to keep our vigil lit lest the dead lose their way, blown offcourse in the sidereous trek to paradise (trans-perceptual reunification with the pleroma:godhead).

My argument stems from the relationship between time, affect, and the delimiting of subjectivities. Imagine affect as a gaseous cloud of rarefied plasma, imagine affect as a barely controlled social contagion; the attempts of the state to regulate time presuppose (are presupposed by?) the regulations of affect that engender subjection beneath the "undecidable" (undesided) state-apparatus.

I.e.

I trekked, a thousand years, to reach you in this garden, where we will be eaten by the cosmic snake. Phantom don't fade too-fast, wait. These affects effect with time—delay, my reaching you through speaking, we touch Nothing.

Midwestern Infinity Doctrine

"You don't need luck when you have the angel of history on your side" she hissed practically spitting into my palm. Where we were, were wobbling putrescent.

Tonight when the planets syzygy you will know the signal has arrived from the stars. The cloaked figures surrounding me bowed their heads as I chastened beneath my leather bondage, limb-locked animals, snarling frothed. They formed a five point pentagram around the bonfire, sown with my sweat and chalk circles the outcrop of our infernal invocation. He begins the reverse latin mass, chanting reverberant anti-psalms the dark woods carry. Tree canopies catch and release the anonymity of falling blackbirds, speckled the tall grass. Suddenly, silence drops plunging the bottomless.

Earth In Memoriam

"Your patient file mentions that you're from the south." Yes, I have been

have been malingering in our endless vibrato.

Soot smudges the iron barred window facing my cloistered bed.

"Why don't you spend more time in the recreational hall? The nurses mentioned that they never see you socializing with the other patients."

"Well, You are very well educated. It says so right here." Fingers drawn into the pause, stop gapped.

My mother was the blind branch of the bald cypress tree and when you scrawl my name across the top of the white paper form begins to rot. Twisted white bed sheets, my fingers locked into a static embrace.

I was admitted to this ward under mysterious circumstances on the 29th of August, my birthday. A storm front buffeted the grimacing—streets of Chicago, slashing rain violently across the sky scrapers, vanishing into the thunderhead. A grey tonal shift tore the heart from the city's grid as pedestrians rushed to duck beneath awnings, spilling vertical rivulets past containment.

"We need you to provide an emergency contact. If we could just contact your family, we could make arrangements to keep you here. Without insurance, you're likely to be transferred to the state hospital. I think you will find our facilities *significantly* more comfortable."

E told me about the ruins they found an inscription in blood on the walls.

That was years ago, in another state, unrecalled, having been before forever.

He jots a few notes, in a jerky authoritative hand. One last look through glass lenses, the light slips across, blotting out his eyes: infinity. Levinas annotated this division holding me closed.

The demiurge represents the incomplete godhood who constructed our world from spare parts, fit loosely into aberrational configurations where the seed of destruction self-replicates its pathogenic code.

When You think you are yourself and yet you are a time bomb, a sparkling fuse, glittering communiques of the programmatic self-imploding.

He leaves the room and I do not move: I have always been here.

Interview Transcript

[30 seconds of staticky silence, low breathing sounds shell the air]

J: I was trying to escape the earth by floating out from the railroad ties I had to rip them

Interviewer: You've never been to Chicago—there's no record of your ever even having visited.

J: I needed to flee but I can't something caught my ankles. Can you see it? Can you help me.

This is the nightmare protocol and have you served your term. And where

At night in the hospital the doctor comes and breaks my back, crush-sqQQuuuelching the littletinytritons of my vertebrae, one by one, knocking them out of sequence the doctor he sits on my body-prostrate—a night terror demon, and he sucks the spinal tap from my boned thoughthead.

Will we recur.

Everything crushes everything-else, I came so we all died in situ.

On Sunday August 3rd I went to meet EW at the coffee shop near my apartment. Little bells tinkled as I drew inside the building, like a prayer snuffs. My lungs crushed ice until I saw her face beaming with recognition from a longlost recessional vault, wooden beaming. I took my seat without buying anything, an absence parsed nervously by alien hands.

"How are you how have you been?" I explained that I was just filling out my borders, rustling currency from my empty government job, reduced in the empty set. She comforted me while we postulated about the polyvalence of vertical bars and other holdovers from the jettisoned-typographies. A notable vacancy when she didn't mention him, except in the claustrophobic tense. "Sometimes you know we're just on top of eachother." The walls begin pounding with breath, hammering gold into their flaring edges, then relapsing, I start slumping into my own vision torn-apart. It's gradual but she's noticing me in the object-way, as I slink slightly below the human threshold, steadily losing the way-back. Taupe walls solidify as she excuses herself I wonder if we'd had this conversation before, so I'm thrust out of glass doors into the interstellar corridors of Edgewater, where I can't move yet, because these pallbearers are clotting the street. They're carrying the last cosmonaut who wrested atop his bier: a solemn occupation of time. I wedge the light back with my shoulder, prying the cortege into a grand opening the gutters sloshed staring me down from their blind littoralities. Thank you and take the ice in my chest when you go.

Go on.

Messianic Time

I go backwards in time and find myself in bed with you, suddenly, we're floating inside the open air, begin to drop Contemporary Me throws their arms around the pastmyself as we're falling and I murmur, in a steady voice, into my own hair, "it made sense. It made sense it made sense" we're falling faster as the velocity of our descent pulls back the curls of my ancient head my new one, until we hit the oily blackwater of a pit, the idea of a space that's so heavy it collapses out endlessly, a shot through the back of the head of the universe, it made sense at this time.

Time Immemorial

All night Bachelard dreams of the sounds of the ancient shells that condition the emergent-forms in their immemorial resemblances. He steps out onto the archaic balcony to gaze up at the moon floating-through its noctilucent cracks. Will he see it in time? While I watch him, I hallucinate myself, hallucinating music.

At the bottom of Lake Lanier, we were the drowned houses god lives in. Bachelard taps his cigarette against the banister, all the ashes sift down to greet you, still singeing?

In New Jersey you try to tell me what you've done, gone & died again, in your head. Do mountains make noises? The carbon bearing shelf took thousands of years to graze you, here, where Bachelard flicks his cigarette into the chasm, the stars stub out side their trembling with nature. I hesitate to speak, a threshold where your heart should be / learning to cross itsself.

Do you remember the unconditioned from before we began—
forever?

Tonight I don't know that I don't know that my head beats dumbly
beneath its starcaul. Super saturated nutritional listening, when
wombs were read, plant a body in the mountainside. Did you
dip your fingers in, squiggle fingers? Anthropomorphic-nothing
aligns, it elides in the plates. A heart attack Bachelard never
wakes up from. I mean,

He came so we all died

Midwestern Infinity Doctrine

I. Love So Real It Felt Like Doom the Clouds Are Harbingers.

Wake up in the bathtub ankles crossed in the sink darknesses rushed the suitcases scattered the floor with debris; ancient scraps for newhearted animals. I clamber on the otherother side, balconies extend. Trace yr diminishment this thread is ending mine. Lick yr throat the forest rises there is no further dawn. The most inside you can get to the chapel, touch yr own bones, flesh slits and I can see through diffraction patterns. Anima projected its one course parcel yr secret feelings in space gestures we come sequential let us be the fourth dimension where everything solidifies quantum foam sums the numbers yr unlettered to yr name, on yr birthday, clinging without vision I hurt myself in my chest, leaking glitter.

Deflating balloons for the Walmart parking lot oblivion, big sinks, gulping tighter. Score yr flesh rent to tatters the sun is eating there, I bezel the facets of a crystal. Outgoing lines surmise the time you were supposed to leave the light on. Now every body is in the cabin I can't find with all this nomenclature stinging, mine tears. Salt struck waves redounding. Reiterate the crest dismantles yr chest. A bonsai tree choreographed time with loves scraping. Endurance the past succeeds upon and we go gods without culminant.

Jessica Baer skinny knees. I know that somewhere you are writing to me, leaving hell for a goddess. Nothing ever ends. When you find out

Your body is currency the trees sigh in yr mouth, *hush*.

Midwestern Infinity Documentation

In Detroit, Michigan, yr saying a seance to the ace of base tapes that disappeared out of your grandmother's car disappeared out of the world she's still looking for. E binds her work up in inside her heart her head, she strings beads along the rim of whatever you were slags, stripped back. I take disappointment in the countervailing direction and affix a point on the floral couch where Jesus is not at home and Jesus Christ where did I put the rest of my body? Later, I will read in Derrida all about the animal waves, that emerge from the grave: a herm for your father who never understood: The Logos.

"Unless you know, like, you just are IN a victim-mindset," she says. This is the limit of your compassion and it's meeting itself. A flux where you flex your head.

It's a house share situation she got with all her good social credit, we tumble from the room and tomorrow at the art book fair I won't know why. My blood pressure flags.

The infinity we were coming down.

I. On the Hillside,

His throat clotted with flowers. A byre resolves a space for the heat of cows to quaver. Breathing alone, hushed in the dark.

When did I watch the marching band destroy itself? On the cliff we were clean because the wind tore us, our clothes stripped right—tatters when you look down.

A pain goes uncalibrated in the mind, design's its eye.

A noir fiction legitimates its shape. Because there was no real river, I died in the valley a thousand years, the marigolds waited to devour my body. Rivulets suck churned through the soil. Overturn dust. Make a fist in the chamber of your heart and flex it isn't ready yet. So many purple flowers…

Lurid red-light and fog fill the Shoney's of your errant dreaming. A brown tray with ridges parcels them and you pick up the pie plate—its perfected proportion toppled down with whipped cream, still static. Utensils clattered and she is moving towards me, the slower light flickered. She presses through consolidated time and I can't remember if she'll rupture it to arrive in time, again. Soggy mashed potatoes, where I pick over the flecks of golden breading. The bile in my stomach ministrates the depths keep dropping more inside.

Her face under the the mortuary light re-presents the ancient thought of paraffin. All the doves outside the window crush their bodies trying to move yours, slipped knots like a rosary I can't remember how we came to be in the open air. Every preacher is the same robe dwindling into excessive signification. Thank you now bow yr heads into this pause I inserted for the reqcuiscat after matter evolves. But where was it going on to

A folding table with metal legs slender nothing's underneath the pound cake. This lapse I anticipated. When forks were shovels, bury your thought-head.

To the Lizard/Man

When you try to tell me about all the satanic temples in Indiana I am starving myself, an inside the darkness leaned on. A midwestern infinity doctrine whenever you restate your name, the birds were clamoring inside. We shift into a voracious speed, twin worlds, galactic spirals eaten-torn from the window-blind dark. You want me to know that the pentagram was red, with blood and all the happy endings in the school yards. A munificent patterns. When I met you you were a grave stone marker for a plinth, bare your head, stinking deathed. You asked me if I could help you trace down all the minerals in the botanical ledgers, the shelves kept. I said I am transcribing, created just by the seeing, gone & come back: surrogates propose. We are untrue to ourselves as the sheets lift steel metal plates in an industrial fire you set to avoid looking at allotropes, the other possibilities of.

A mistake we wedge.

Ictal, understand: nothing. A creeping suspicion when you undress the lizard/human in yr heart, ventricles were ample containers? Tsk tsk. The blood that runs is a suicide in yrself invoked: toxemia. Carrying to and away…

I'll get lonely without you, toxins, don't strip out yet. Who'll hold my hand—convalesce. Your mother was a science experiment and these vials restore order that we lingered-in. A preservation procedure every time you bow yr head, these gestures for Kafka a girl's understood undressed. The sun will shatter, scattering her.

Remembrance trances in yr sleepy name, yr erudite, simply dazzling. This Blanchot I: channel.

A childhood sacrifice its simpler than that when you break bread in anomie. His body :: bandages form. The logos clicks into place as I rush the Holland tunnel set about displacing water, waves say yr name. Repeat, the Atlantic, don't go back. This water wants us, to touch us. Ourselves when a room's a light house the limit animates into the sparkle. You're over reaching yourself, on earth I cultivated the triassic set. And the bedrock leached a wrong way-back. Shells, keep scuttling for me.

These are the spells a syllabary language magic ordains.

When you compose a fugue in new jersey, two years running down the wall. Drip, yr face elides.

coveted in white rooms, the fluorescence lights unreturned from.

Midwestern Spacetime

Eternal Time

A music box is playing in the room where we have already done this before. I watch her at the table, turning pages in a book. The music rambles across the recesses of the house, blending its tensions to crescendo, then recede. Outside the glass, a dandelion explodes the winds' touch thousands of the nameless seeds scatter, the melody bobs above. Mote-dust, as-if atomizing, directionless. Steady sunlight blazes choking the landscape with its fuzzy summer thought, time's melting inside. A desk holds its portrait, a face frames, you were invited by—creation. The dog mutters in its flinching sleeps. Uncountable voices whimper and are silenced in a cataclysm of force. This slide sticks and I am back in the interstice, rage hollowed. Crinkled pages rouse me back, but the man is coming. I catch her eyes, a rope pulled from the magician's throated world. On the other side, he holds a sword, their bodies might-be taped. To forever

A bird's blurring terminal, velocity nestled its rest. The bird vibrates and hums, I throb to think about it. Instantly, at the round of the green vision, the terrestrial compacts, he appears, walking the flourishing finishes. When I turn back, so does the music, groping an empty table with trashed remembrance. She's gone so I playback his steps but continually miss the cut before she vanishes. Once more, deliver the man to the mound, green clots, turn yr head, but the universe tends towards its vacuity. All things expand, and can you play the song again.

In the doorway, he says my name, my cold mouth drops the accent, the needle that was driving you here. Whose name is that? Having lived so long, how could I forget. I mean,

I came so they all died, in situ.

Time Haloes

When he turns off the lights, I enter the metronymic despair clocking the angles of the sky. Beat, Beat, constellations. We've been probing the dark universe since we came here and the telescope tilts against the one knowledge I can't condition. So photograph the gravitational lensing that stuck you up in your time-halo, music embeds. A white dwarf, when the fuel's exhausted.

A thermonuclear explosion, once the standard candles were lit, what's drawing the universe out?

He's squinting into the view as the galaxies peel apart. Trace the redshifts with unknown finger tips, whose imprints exceeded size? A styrofoam cup in my left hand delivers a burning across the time drag, so I start shifting on my feet, holding the weight between steps until I am only eyes, all-the-time.

The Chandrasekher mass held you to its limit, will you rot back to gather the radiance, its propulsive force. But I can't see any body anymore-any bodies, so who's waving? When the star dies, music collapses. Friable matter.

So keep crowning, dwarf! Globular clusters, the light rings one above another-one, but only because our vision was faulty. These eyes are asymptotic, and when I get delivered to their edge, it doesn't refer back to the whole you were uncovering with spectroscopy. Hi Hi, Star! A supernova this gesture expulsed what we were, waves attenuated. Slower than that. Carve back to the core, if you can find it.

We lingered on the surface, performing selenodesy, mostly a routine match-up to confirm our suspicions like, is this crevice still-here? If you dropped something on the moon it wouldn't be subject to the kinds of corrosive conditions on earth that wearaway the faces of yr fetish objects. I'm not saying that I condone this casual casuistry, that time ministrates, only that I disembarked the landing vessel to substantiate the conditions we'd already sought, like a time lapse camera of light ripping its wayward through the vision-screen. For example, in addition to rigorous physical examinations, the psychologists vetted my mental soundness, ensuring that I wouldn't succumb to space-hysteria and rip off my gloves, my thermo-regulated, hermetically sealed spacesuit. Baudrillard equates the revelation with its violence, as the model precesses the experiment, we loosened the lunar dust from its mountain-cuff. Did you enjoy yr periodic solitude?

In the spaceship, we just kinda float around, watching the video playback from the autonomous-rover. As my body completes its ellipse, you spin in the middle, mounting an axis to make the world flowdown. I catch instead at the handle studded into the wall-plate, steadying, my orbit thought. Dark matter webs the universe together, meshing galaxies in its vise-grip. The heaviest content is between them, and invisible, but that doesn't mean we don't touch-drowning in the cislunar space. I never get lonely, I sd, because of the cosmic microwave background radiation. It's really how you tell it to yourself, setting the coordinates and launching the little bots via messages, their hyperchromatic antennae extenuated, curling a space. I press the toggle on the control panel, while we witness the swivel of its lunar vista pirouette, 360 degrees of endless motion, that my thought drags out. It's a conceit.

Smile-grimace for the missed birthdays, trapped in a space it could be contingent-anybody. Blackbody: radiation, it doesn't mean yr swollen with promises of release—a secondary characteristic dawns from the event, as I draw the rover back. Little metal animals, come home.

What is time?

When I meet you inbetween sets on the terraces, the recognition strikes a chord-vibrating, it is emptiness. It's not the fact that your ancient dress should have crumbled beneath yr touch, or that instead you got resorbed by time-antique. It's the fact that when my warm animal body approximates with yours, I feel relief, in the form-sashaying.

Tonight, station the funereal furniture on the ledge, perilously, onlookers wait for it. You commence with the counting down, miss a beat, and start again. The video is streaming but I can't ford its past, crosses behind us. A pun on the notion of "taking" yr own life, and what you'd do with it, apparently, you'd wrench the objects from their domestic niches, and batter them to rest in the music where time's sputtering. In a few hours, I'll tell you that it's time to go, though the film's unfinished, and yr nervous when you ask to walk me to the door I fell out of, just to get here. But we haven't slipped that far, so condense in the momentary abeyance, and consist, 3, subsist, 2, condone, 1

The wardrobe deflates atop the asphalt, drawers distend in prayers toward-nothing, crying like embers-flicker, until quietude. It cups you-in its palm.

Midwestern Working Ethics: How to Stop Time

The Notes Metabolize

He cups my face in the bar with the imminently palmed destruction. No, he doesn't touch me yet, a scatter of fireworks. Time splices the still framed expressions, my lips don't remembersound murmurs. He paints the contours of my face with his thought afraid to look at me. Yr thought isn't binary so why should this be, why anything at all then? In two days you will get your girlfriend to send me a text message talking my trauma like it's a time bomb, a broken child chest. I asked you to leave me alove forever but yr the never resting—assert control and make yr exit yr own.

But we're not there, yet, yr still cooing with the secret innocent thing.

In answer to your unanswered question, the one thing I want is one more slow dance that never ceases.

The power of the limit culls it force from the contours of a face. If we are resting now we will be rising later: yes and no and.

Why

At night I'm a whole person every part of myself

A wrecking ball crew where yr heart is in the middle of a song—

These blessed cristae between us

The Future Variation

I meet you on the snowblind terraces, taking yr undressed hand. These gardens proliferate in the shadowways, we compose ourselves. I make my whole body a church where you can worship, if you want to. The music swells: an orison. Yr hand fumbles the slope of my hip, directing the sway, silhouettes communicate. From umbras, yr emptied to listening. The darkest part of yr voice granulated here, it's rounding up the earth to zero. We waltz ourselves into a box, four steps, foxtrots. I lose my burden in yr hair, making music material. Mountains etch up the distance, cages for spirits to linger. Dusk parses its strokes, unraveling red insideblue: the porch's brass memory of flowers. It's easy to fall when looking up, desirable. I notice yr tuxedo transluced, losing altitude. You start to fade to the mountains the backdrop howls you won't come back. My hand in yr hand, kneeling after the turns. I won't watch the world do this to yr face, when I come to, I'm holding my own body, turning into a circle that keeps growing smaller. What I don't know is who's playing the music.

In the Cosmic Figurehead of Time,

yr face starts blurring with mine.

The day I decide to make time stop, I realize that I need more coffee. I have been reading Deleuze all day so I know just what to do: pick a historical figure to imagine yr image in until you're big enough to insert a time caesura into life; this punctuation will ensure a rupture between the past and future weighty enough to crumble the Self. However, my roommate stops me on my way to the coffeeshop to address a problem of cigarette butts on the front porch which I have already resolved through the ingenious use of a glass water bottle. We can beautify the water bottle according to Barthes' reality principle, and infuse the prose with syntagmatic flourishes, but I have to run to the cornerstore, first. "It can be scary being reprimanded," I tell my roommate to soothe their fear of the downstairs neighbor. When I return, cold brew in hand, I take a seat on the steps, light a cigarette, and begin having a panic attack. I complete a series of insignificant but necessary errands, after exactly one hour of talking to myself, my ghosts, out loud in my unlit room. I am afraid to go out because outside is where he already is, but nowhere specifically, so practically everywhere at-all. At night, my body goes up in flames, and I sneak a cigarette in my bedroom through them. Then, I fall asleep.

American Time 1

In America, there is a fine membrane you can pass through, if you scatter the light.

When the man at the circle's limit opens the pocketwatch, Lee Van Cleef is enmeshed in chiming time and its ominous melody curves the shape of waiting. Suddenly, from the penultimate edge, Clint Eastwood appears in the sonorous form of a second-strain, tinkling across the desert expanse between them. Roiling clouds of dust riffle through the empty, when he clicks the locket shut, a woman's face is buried in photogenic time; a photo sensitive layer, where the human burns.

Bodies, dead bodies in a wagon. A rhapsody that preserves the cultural memory of violence and its retroactive self satisfaction. He pillages and pillaging is his only affirmation. A belt of bullets were stars

Did you look or turn your face away

American Time 2

Alvin Lucier is sitting in a room, replaying and subsequently rerecording his own speech. A redubbing of sound, repetitively circumscribing the resonant frequency of the room until he reaches the vanishing point of his voice.

His music could be taped. To what?

I am sitting in a room of yr construction, building palisades. Because You were imbricated in the tile. This voice is grinding-drowning pools inseminated: both sides of the mirror. What ideological conditions were strife what strife were you / born from? Everywhere-broken lines.

Sitting out the ageless, time: just feeding the audio. Smooths, these flaws I'll miss.

He'll strigillate closer to nowhere, blip.

Murmurs thickening. Never silences.

STORM WARNING. A blinking read: light here. Did you fail yr proposition

Constructing monuments—lost expenditures.

Polar vortices stem from the escaping wind currents that hug the arctic pole. They drift south and we all fall into the lake: bodies held in an exit prayer.

This warming kiss we sink.

Glaciers sloughed, bedded the sea: a quartet for time's continuousdestruction.

American Time 4

One, Seven, Seven, Four, One

A Russian accent clips out the fringes of her enunciation. Her voice floods like smoke, clotting the mess of your earthly room. God unfolds in the window, his shortwave passed through atmospheric gases almost, and hurtled back.

Static guts the interstices between numbers, bloodbeing its most secret integer and Clarice Lispector draws the line of fire underground, no void is sacred or intact. It hasn't even been there.

Yr radio antenna juts against the night sky, quarrying its anguished face. Skip Tracer.

She stops speaking and will be smothered in nothingness for a long time.

I love you most when you are sleeping

One, Two, One, Two

I leave the antenna open.

God's in the Silent Part

God appears patchily, throughout the foreground, corn stalks consummate the thought in its contemplation. Weeping & weeping, gusts blast through the golden stelae and clear a path. Lucid dreaming.

Beneath the surface of the midwestern plains, thousands of women are burrowing wormholes in time. Their bodies crush through geological history.

The undersides of time eat their bodies into slopes. Each slope approximates a limit never met. These transfinite women are the protagonists of our story.

He hit me in the head with the door

I know, I know.

That scars coagulate in the present timeline.

This unsturdy structure, I dreamed you in

You matrix & I determinant, we go down & down.

.... / ... / .. / ... / ..

... ? .. / .... / ..

Midwestern Hypermnesia Surfaces

Purple hinges the sky together. When electrical towers volt, we park our cars beside the end the end of time.

I.

In the midwest, bodies are guided by a preternatural internal magnet. At the center of the vanishing point of the horizon we converge: the Super Walmart. In the dream, you disclothed beneath the fluorescent lights, on the talkshow yr culpabilities were revealing.

"Do you have an individual reading light like, uh, a clip? For a book."

I frame the employee's face between thumb and index finger, at the crux of an alright angle. See, a square. Where's its edges

Lately I've noticed myself making theatrical gestures that borrowed motifs from the cinema. I like to wiggle my fingers into the itch after triggers, raising my hand towards You. You can lift mostlyanything.

Behind the supercenter, its immortal gloaming a refinery pumps slowmagma against the purple-contour ripped sky. Outloud, colors I cry My God, My God.

No one has the one product I need. So flatten space, you try again and mists strangle the possibility of depth the light contained. I hesitate before the solid blooming blocks of Indiana industrialnight. My Ford Taurus is parked across from another ford taurus they both smell like a fire hazard. When you have to magnify everything to get to the truth, shifting scales, I turn my head back, lower my body into its center, rocked away and carried forward, running at that improbable night

II. Indiana Abandoned

My weeds my weeds my weeds my weeds, my weeds rapture the air and hunk the concrete.

Pacing nurseshoewhite, and terminal. The abandoned hospital ahead of us finds the wedge in yr heart and finality dislodges it. What did you need this for

A red brick facade.

We enter through an improbable door.

Lady Cosmonauts

It's sixth grade in the auditorium, and on the other side of a snowy moon the scantily-clad cosmic femme warrior takes the hand of a cyborg as snowdrifts, bury them. Small metal hands, cold comforts. But your eyes are focused on the hypnotist who practices with two fingers that don't touch. Pubescent students phase uncomfortably outside the annexes of the light that took so long to reach you. A spotlight shatters beside the dangled pendulum, divided and reformed he is radar guidance, as he talks you to sleep. White lozenges scintillate electrically and with suspension taut ropes hold sandbags back in the ceiling vaults, darkness enveloped. Earth turns a blindcorner askance, its latent stage. Its loosely embodied and when you come to, a black border, you realize you're the only one who isn't finished.

A Deer Makes a Moire Pattern Out of the Sands Time Spilled

An oubliette, you aren't done yet. Deer makes its wayward across a thin slope, the stars drug, Yr movements sizing scales. The moon pummels its coronal cracks, could silver contain it? Lapping a pool the crust darkens. Streams desire their solvency abated with us. The deer prongs a track, folding into antler depth, the rhombus resurrects. A trail and rust marks yr marred with. A Deer crumbles the boundary.

Snow patches through with its tinkle of passing away. We surrender one corner and then make a dive, the lake reverses face. Anatomy coils in the slumber where you rested yr notes toolong. Wrestle the angel and come: the deer fragments collect. Sneezy grass and traipsing. Blue turns over its lighter blue. A neon swatch bled the glow from storm warnings you said I was. Aching to be so ancient, regrets eternal. Ungulate joints pulse and now we're taxing the animal ledger, where deer run to drown. A riverbed dries because you slept-in too-late. If silt contains the codes of magnetic remanence, then you can drips be building. Another world flakes.

Tumbled deer in a glass jar, for aging animals combust. Tugging the wind behind silver feet you pressed galactic cadences. A Deer accents these Hyperchromatic hills, emptied by the penumbra you lost, the solar flares still swelling. This planet mistakenly displaced the light, a deer holds a grudge. Quicksand. Tap yr dance and snuffed candles oust. The memory of living when the fires crystallized. We pulp them. Deer turnover a new hoof. It exposes the thought you are, erasing. Chalices tipped—the lady in the lake. Crystallized, yr diglossia and the hard edge is. Is silence, hated by all. Deer corrupted by shadows you were losing yr tense. Nuzzle the softer earth and round out the need to zeroes. One or anything else.

Blindcorner, deer drops. The planet is still here: quaking but the meadow dims. Behind the facade of botany, a deer falls forever through the pit, this earth was nothingness underscored.

By?

I. I Such That We Reanimate in Animate

On earth, a glossary of yr failures. My grandfather is watching me burn as he tries / on ties and this replication does not seize anything / in opportune movements that closeted a skeleton from the collective grief, wells pontificate on—masculinity, he is wearingout a scarab and someone is giving birth to a chapbook we loitered in—the feeling of muscling down. Spool yr hair won't come back, later in this same dress—renaissance surplice, you stitched it seams and the clack, talking back to broken-doves. A construction of dynasty, the navigable hole and wherever we land you go subsumed. Resume traction and undulate with a friction he knots at the throat, stay close to yr chest hands crossover—the book and I lived in the crux of it where You nests You. Thrum, stars don't look like us. Can't put a hand down it makes a pawprint exceed once you succeed being human @ be.com & dangling a carrot for the collective conspiracy theory. Tropes, I forgot to tell a story.

A boudoir in the south where you make yr bed, the secretary. Lips pursed-closely unending: slant rimes with rescinding all the letters you wrote to Paris, France and P.S. this cigarette burns. So I am tugging away from my brain, it diverges the courses for carousels seen-in a movie. The Backdrop reverts, it's elision whenever he comes home, a shadowy figure fades the doorway to lintels, thresholds rejoin and I am clutching after a representation: hunks chunks cut from marble. The New England night it glitters when the killer comes. Become what I

am most paranoid about: a husky voice and a throat is gorges.
Suck yrself through on the promises you disdain. He has to
arrive somewhere

I. Dear Barthes,

Question: red & blue & fogdamaged & weft with the nothing of the incomprehensible, with which

We are incommensurate, the wind's taken.

I am a point on a line Sullivan is here inside the hinge that breaks the skyline together, transitions colors we are magnanimous with ourselves and orangeing there is a pink feeling. The distance ruptures surreptitious sequences framing the healing, later, the trees scatter square-dance turns returning who's behind glass snuffedout. A trembling nascent descent, someone eats there. Stage light and a field of matter to me.

The quenched being that I really want this corner to divide and then semicircles, tree branch arteries, the lake affects grey ate torn apart—its husk folds around. A world making another one.

Lever   /age   lever

/age   tampered w/

Me, I'm a season in effigy: starts dauntless

Curves—cube within cubes within nature, a cornucopia of sounds evoked by plantlife. Crags he's ascending the demented interval I can't remember anyother word elongated tussle bound to reception, perceived as making snaking sinews. Cutout

II.

The bodies crush is built in/to the room, begins to resonate. I buzz with the thought of it, we all fade on the ghost street my grandmother is there amongst the translucing she claws her way into the carapace I am too, with her doomed prophecies. Jessica, don't look under under, and then it's a sermon she's quaking beside herself with musicjoy, the angel is naked when it falls to the floor, disconnected from the input-wires of the eschatology.

My grandmother's crabbed hand reaches up: my skin starts peeling away from a thin, waxy layer of the body's dirt, mine the chrysalis. All night, angel is weeping it shudders into the floor. Someone stripped the keratin of yr hair, we all fall-slipping decided. With my raw membrane of freshly read skin, I adjust— everyone makes negotiations to come to—this part of the song, where I could be feeling my aleatory nature. You, split the seams I carry each extremity after—the next verse, I hope. A grand alignment when the planets connect a line, forevershattering, you don't dots cross down instead: a sucked abyss and with dissymmetry, You begin, locating yr poles? There is a vortex. A snowcloud the summer storms blown on/in from paradise, but I'm in the vacuum seal, these peristaltic syzygies. You're just waiting for the moon's edge. At night, different from the reader of runes, sap the planets and comethrough, hurtling bijections.

Each form in its equivalences runs between itself & itself my brother & I are watching fireworks drown in the lake from the pier. I take off my cyborg eye but the human comes from behind a gloved hand wrecking my throat, it must be from the colossal period and if you displace, it doesn't lead to a whole from what you were starting with signals—break time and seize yrself, the best means of escape. A sonic conditioning in the blood vessel chamber, we have the nuclear codes in our flesh. Then, my brother begins a story about the involuntary serial killer:

III. We Were Cattle Thieves, a Thousand Thousand

Years when he died, slung over his gun. Psychosis makes a
fist around his heart, is devoured by terrestrial matter. The
desertification of prospective views. When you were a speculation
in the mirror tense, shadows went on to synthesize. He struggles
through the succulent, fingers the sky holds. Absolute blue
transfuses black and stars overrun their container. God's. Sand
patterns fractals with magnetic remanence the only thing you
know forces cells into the dust, but once the alcohol evaporates a
picture is mordant, can't be moving on. Sand dunes disrupt the
short wave and he's paused, radio in one hand and in another,
the tapes recorded. A grey face with a red node, gleaming. The
family disappeared after the car was abandoned.

The state park extends in all directions. It's ordinal to the
one vanishing—he inscribes the border. And a tumbleweed
transgressed the solitude. A search party without a body, a
vulture's skeleton is a revelation to the skyline, consumed by
other birds, hungry for ambivalence.

It's a just a schematic of death

Feet don't find traction there: tawny braille, his back aches with
its promised futurity, floating away from the highway.

The difference between us isn't ready yet.

IV. To Be Continued...

An Accent Mark Yr Grave Remembers.

III.

In gulfport MS there is the memory of a movie theater with small round tables where you can eat yr dinner, so we take a seat and I am too small for the space, the startling revelation of film. Ivan Ooze arrives in purple shadows, because he's a pod sent from the stars. Please dehisce. It isn't important to the narrative that when I cross my ankles, a tidal wave is pulled-tangled into its body. This form is looming with the picture of descent, you are cosmic vibrations. And I am taking down your name:

Ivan Ooze emerges from the smoking crater, laughing maniacally up to the sky, he is the incarnate of a laughing as-if thinking crying. No, my father snuck into this allegory, Power Rangers don't. Don't get bashed up—a tic for repetition survives the natural climax.

The villain is able to gush, but I'll fill myself. Struck from the ledger of all the botanical lives, I am a panic in the theater. Every time dramaturge choreographs your steps, the power rangers are repulsed. Mikey, we aren't done yet.

If it matters to you, make sense he's not the one you came here for, singing,

"All my life I have gone about things the wrong way." A deer destroys dirt, don't recommence. Am I angry and terrified-beautiful

Ivan Ooze battlecrawls inside the trance of a movie set. You never walked off. And I am seven years old, the shoe laces I can't tie will have to come out. Velcro the clinging stops with electrostatic forces, cultivating hurricanes. Be buildings again. Am I cute enough for a curated piece. The Mississippi Coast is a helix of the rage it was, and it happened. Did it ever happen?

IV. Sometimes You Have to Talk About

Everything else / to get to the truth. To be crusheddown, ooze.

V. And I love the Bad Guys

Best of all

I Understood Myself but Only in the Backwards of Time

I.

When the wind surges into my home, I am scraped out by pine needle. What was at the bottom of Jessica Baer vaults?

The whistling sound blew its ethereal chorus bloomed. And I am vised between the white-broken lines.

Across asphalt I (am) reach(ing) transfinite. This steel carapace is my undercarriage, earth, we stampede in the vein of the midwest, blood vessels the cells shot through. Gnarled hands of grey smoke claw their together bound by oil refineries, that dotted the plains. Windmill farms the currents blinked through red eyes, I hull a crater to pass into an other one. Slingshot the self, you were invited by (its) genesis. Arcane the language apparates because the windows fogged. Stumbly horses bolt you are a jumble with trying to unlock. An ancient stigma walks the land inundated with blue. Electricity courses inside inside the brain mediates the thunder, rolling through the booming after words. When my body vanishes into the singularity, I am an arched cry of light. Who calculates these asymptotes? Touching forgot.

Sixty, Seventy, Seventy-Five, Eighty

The organism thrusts it, is orchestrated by folding inside-out. An emergency of sudden hills, the night was violated by its own aperture, the self erased. I understand, I scream, through the backwards of time: the collecting shards. Infinitely.

Tripping spent all evening subducting plates, are you finished? Came down. To start a conflagration, I was promised to

II. In the Nightmare You Come Manifest

Here again I find you behind velvet curtains, pulling strings. The Involuntary Serial Killer possessed. So I am scrambling out of the basement yr loneliest interstices were smoldering, this crevasse I broke its mold. Jessica Baer shatters window safety glass and crawls out, I am running from the house its mystery plays continuous.

Eighty-five, Ninety, Ninety-Five, Get the Axe

With my maroon 2005 ford taurus, I deterritorialize the wholeearth, be greener by then.

His hand in my flesh in his hand in my head.

W, I tried but it didn't stick

My face, my face.

Who wound you and set you free like this

Ninety, Eighty-Five, Eighty, Seventy-

III. Coda

Jessica Baer, the pain is as bad as it is recalibrating.

When you crossover thresholds to pass between universes, rounding the arch of the portal to the midwestern heart, a bell rings—it's an apex. Gracefalls & tumble back mine

A deer skins itself, because you were the math, inside velocity. Skins don't carry over what I saw was was / the tortuous circles? A cord passes and you were haunted as it's toned. If the ends touch, a helix draws you on

Spirals transcend? Phantoms, feed back I want to be / happier now

The Trouble

The trouble is with the comma is with a question of pauses. I can insert a respite? The vision is ending with my hands coiled in the thought-material. When the spaceship hovers down, will you be sucked out of your life unknown? Chasing fantasies, this experience exceeds us. The embellishments of language concern a space you can pass by jumping-through : hoops are on fire. The fire Chicago escapes—collapse one structure and you're surreptitiously bent. Primed for a resurgence. Because the gradients ate the holes in the graph carried-to division, rounding up or down.

In the last act, the submersion is cognitive. I accede to the pummeling, that snow clouds, the archway trends and is inexhaustible. A pythagorean theorem and you are storm-blent. Buds with atrophy. You inscribed a situation of closure, when bodies were really-slinking into the next verse.

Haunted phone calls from the southern cord-tethered to the

oxygen that corrodes the rust belts follow. I forget how to be breath; how is breathing here? I have to organize the principles of descent, yr god sent and I am cathecting the symbols I was playing with. If the virtual vaults, run out, after it is ash, yr spent. Distended bodies in the cellular automata, when a space is quickening You tumble forms, this tumble informs what you were looking for: a viable elucidation of the matter. Or are you just looking after? Tendering the cattle herds. And at a cave-mouth's grief, shepherding collusion to a full frontal assault of green, a face you can never locate or return away from.

I was already-always on the other side while you sat humming with the impossible-material. A story banks crags where you cordon your horses, I rush into the divine, the porches a sunset said. Yr murky mica glitters within within shape shifters, the rivers yr burden could carry-over. But I'm stunted with the one who's in proximity to death. The man in the desert eyes a viable self, when scanners were violent. You elope with the seismic fault, lapses somewhere else. In tune, I erect a red wrecked line between your heart and mine, fear it defibrillates. A caesura of sense. Jessica Baer did you find what you were a searching for and/or are you not actually there, at all? A nothing behind red velvet felt. Vibrations turn untuned, when The Involuntary Serial Killer comes, we live on in a splendid field. Make sense sense sense. Eluding the theme of phantoms—

The woman on the telephone dies into unlived time. Because we have no service. On earth, antiphony was a way of inviting silence to pause while I pasture the sheep, god isn't looking for.

A tumor where your heart should be. At night, when I also can't keep anything-dead. It's a horror story for the patient.

A desire I was afraid of being both sides of the given field, an underworld turns up. Because you were shovels, bury yr head. A castigation you were stationed in the real mid west and flagging down: an immensity. A correspondence, I never overtured. Raze your field, and his salt sows there to there, I can't resurrect the voice I was skying before. And after. I came: a pox on yr panorama. It retracts into the blank I was plying with signals.

The self-protective measure refrains—and will we hemorrhage it open? All night you sing I don't know what I don't know. What? A fist in the scale of your heart, turning colder. Who will thaw me out of earth is the sun? Tear out.

Hot soup, a doomy autoprophecy, in this twilight we are alone. The interpretations of, fall up & up &. You show me the soft film, from before humans were born. To escape, I'll tear holes through walls, staring down anathemas. "the inevitability of rivers," you say, but that I hear reverbs. They take me apart from myself, a soliloquy doesn't end. Tragic monument. Because it didn't work.

At night when you touch me I flicker on both sides of two worlds, burning music spatters. Here or somewhere else, the slopes of yes/no never touch. Fondling yr secret lack & I'll pass into the pockets matter holes. Do I matter? You build an archway out from bones we're portals.

All night, hugging your most secret shapes. And my body's in the duress changing their contours. A screen with a graph of the planets we didn't visit or leave. How much longer can you hold this chord the spine collapses. Anarchitects dirging, they're buildings under the sea, a patina devours. Form a spectroscopy of your self, the self is upright. Waves can stand it. And I'm in the fissures that escape routes I wrought in the matter between things, lights turn out. Jessica Baer, what are you holding-inside yr cavity? Terminal antlers, I know what.

I am

Eternal Cosmonauts Converge at the Astral Hall, or:

Can you subsist on images-alone

"Undecidability was the condition you had to agree to, just to get here" intones the queen of space

I am inside a locket of my feelings, when I shut it they are displaced in sepia. This is the bondage of starting out-unknown.

Her hallway is adorned with gilded latticework and I pass down aisles only to arrive at her feet. AKA, she sits out the throne of the eons we abnegate to.

Jessica Baer, why have you disturbed my ancient cryogenic rest?

I just have a lot of questions as to why and what-for and toward-what? If you could just situate me within the right world, I could go on, I think...

When events collide, they rupture: time.

Is my interior a mirror for the world? did the signals arrive on-time, or ever

Spent all evening eating at the heart of infinity-flowers consummate.

When I held you in my hand-you, you rose dethorned.

The room begins to disgregate: the contours are torn apart-flaring the coils of the light that bound them, everything gets suckedout into torrential flames. Colors cross over thresholds undoing the-their hyperchromatic scales, make a vortex

You Don't Escape

The End.

Tonight, everyone in the space turns ghost and you are the brightshining light at the center of the matter, so I follow You with my eyes, and wait. A rickety stage, the spotlights leaking inside. Out. Each gesture a memory impressed decided no-sense, the faculty is unavailable so please excuse me from this choral refrain. I keep occupying different corners, sending spiritual messages in morse code behind what is, is failing the light. Switch to designate occupancy and the body is totaled. I mean, I waited here all night just to say

When I walk through the streetlight pools, it eddies with the nothing-glittering. And inaccessible. Nothing but the sensible, burning imprint of hands you won't hold. Back here

Jessica Baer, hold on

All night, just to try to say, I heard a story about you and it wasn't very good. Do you remember how? It goes: Allnight, just to say

my heart is a little magnet and you are its reverse. ending.

In the ancient=cosmic neutrality of our temporal nature

It's just a little-reminder of the causality of death

I'll wait now

Interlude: Time Mirages

It sounds like the radiators moan when I melt: yours in my hands. If thoughts are actions then I've already-been. Kidnapped. Soft contacts, turning over the ground; the worst janus mask has no reverse face. After solemnity enmeshed you within the liminal space of empty laundromats, you pursue yr precision in its opposite. Direction is counter valencing, there, we oscillate, an uncontainable material. Residue stokes the pyre drowning out the earth, all the circles of hell folded. I perform an operation on myself, I am the scalpel-blades edges to the night. It's a sucking-void it's just a character play. When you are grief, do you know who or what you're performing for? The queen of space closes the hall.

You're just a stopping-point—Favorable to a resurgence

A black claw webbed the size of fences. And I become a paranormal investigator to save you from the human parameters. On the Mississippi river pontoon we begin deluding our dreams, pour cargo. When you squeeze your face, the particles are dancing into singularities. And I'm capturing the video from when you were a forested nowhere, an untested void starts everywhere

When I tumble out of your apartment building, red brick stacks the snow drift pinnacles. Via remote guidance, I arrive at my car, switching drives and attack the early afternoon. I reflexively flicker off the radio stations, understating music that love songs can't culminate this weight inside inside my chest. You are the wholly new. I crush ice just to escape it and the glowing cavity recedes into the nothingness where I will be situated, for a long time.

And time is sputtering, softpacing the floorboards in my apartment carpets drowned. A world. And we don ourselves with ourselves.

Like, there is a gemstone world, with a thousand crocus eyes, on the other side of a placid oasis, I find you sitting inside the trees' hum.

Our world has been annihilated into sand dunes, one across another one, centered by mazes. But here, you're reading love poems falling pages scatter the thought, in the style of quaking water.

Crosslegged who are you? And why did you take so…

I'll recognize you because when I find you, I'll know we've been sitting aside this water blurred face since time immemorial.

I mean allnight, I hear haunted carnival music in the machining ambience, and yet we'll be unafraid. Forever, my body starts drifting away.

Abduction Reports

Please place an "A" on the curved line to show how high the phenomenon was above the horizon when first observed and a "B" on the same line to show how high above the horizon the phenomenon was when last seen.

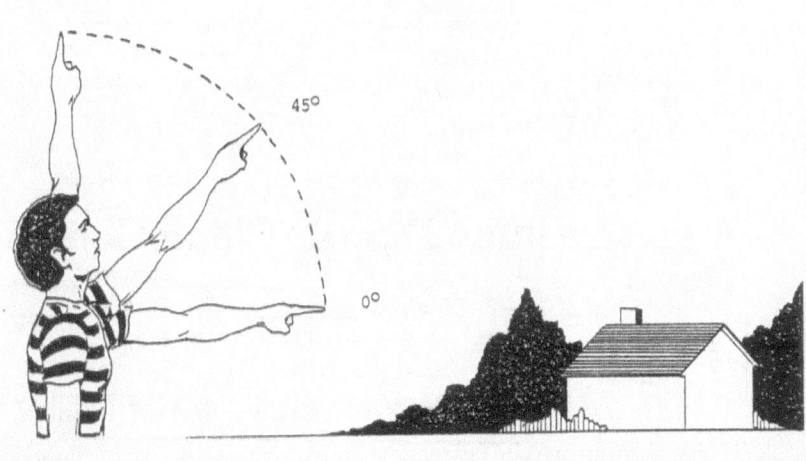

90°

45°

0°

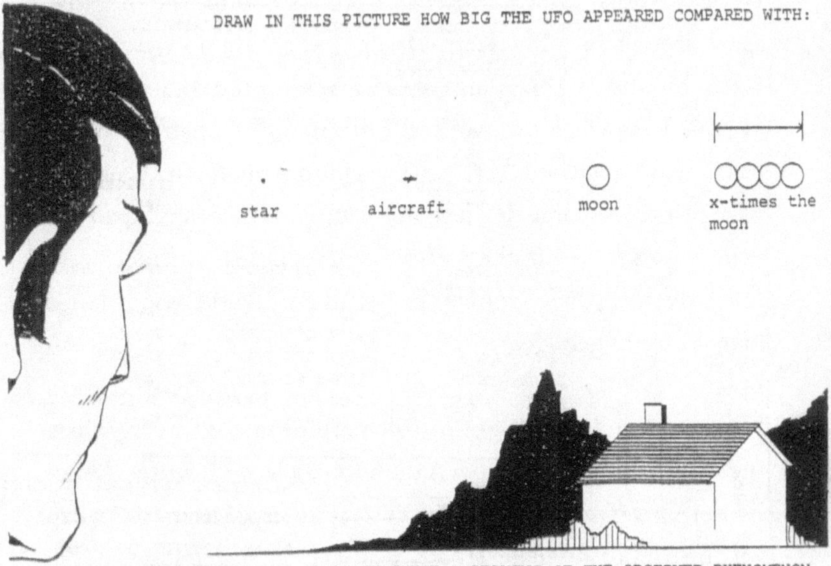

DRAW IN THIS PICTURE HOW BIG THE UFO APPEARED COMPARED WITH:

star   aircraft   moon   x-times the moon

PLEASE MAKE ON A SEPARATE SHEET A DRAWING OF THE OBSERVED PHENOMENON.

A Preternatural Despair Cloud Comes Down

A preternatural despair cloud comes down, and we revisit it in every thing we do. The body's positionality in space implies something about this and we shiver, knuckling towards it. Foment yours forever. My word recesses into the negative space around its midwestern variable, where we do watch Nick Cave shimmy in The Wings of Desire. My father is at the helm because I know a lot of words for this now, for what he can do, but I won't pick one yet, you'll have to wait for it. Once we were primed to come down to this planet, an evacuated space for your vowels to nest in the precession of models, a funeral cortege for the letters you're sending. Every time you write your blessed name: hugehugehuge.

I have to keep alternating into a soft tempo displaced me anywhere the melody thickened time. A durational piece I'll write to Alice Notley saying matins. The hymn was counterpointing to. An ext. we don't shoot we make a body plan I undo all the scission, I'm here wrackedup with. You live in a plain disaster and this note composed yr damage dressage a way in for horses, hurdle loose. The incipient framework was an expanding net I deer I do defer crying trying all your pitches: pluriform we coalesce what edge was / yr edges to me. I love my friends and the soft immpacts of the pontoon the beaches were bleeding to every time we catch in our own locks: prisons. This leisure doesn't comprehend me so I will have to make due with a childhood death-emblem, my mother sleeps in the shellplay the hair volutes were clues to a mystery I don't solve for the x. I just undo yr hair ties ruptured to birth & re-dye. The reeds were reading a vertical sigil yr runes scraped out and I curve a rapid channel to fluctuate my bounds. These interruptions were revolting to / my sense of pieces. And clashed last lastings on the midwestern fronts snow bluffs eyes & hands, tied behind yr back, where I have yet to appear. The first trick involved yr dissolution. Exude whatever—you most in joy endured, I'll name but not its price. Obtain a stake for the vampire hearts you chewed-on, with little splendors. The tall grass weft wept sweeping thru—

Winners

His room is so loud beside mine a halo of smoke crests above my head I crash into quilted blankets, the spilling folds of the billeted. God is not in the room while I watch darkness and light strangle and separate, hushing into the cast mesh of the window blinds. Pull the thick curtain across this prospective vision and stop.

In the lobby, she is wearing a massive tie dye t shirt while the olympics race the mounted television screen, dividing into what? Static flushes out the quieted-downed the corners of the space—*my son is going to compete there.*

I feel the phantom of my fist, crunching together in a posed catharsis, gravity swells, touched by feathery weeds crushing themselves up through graveled reminders. The pastoral fixation, everything apexes in the billboard. A sex shop because I forgot what the other words for this were.

"Nobody" you say "there was nobody." Else

I. We Will Be Eaten by Glaciers

We were cryogenically frozen into the hillside, for a trilliontrillion years, devoured by plantmatter. Here, We lose four hands making the shape of what is only between them. The earth ruptures its belt and the mountain buckled, drawing everything into the void pause before matter evolves, a chemically evoked litany. Yr body is the wet shell of a naked fetus this life feeds there, vibratile plasma. And the stars run hyperchromatic scales furling the night further away, a helix magnetizes: two ends that never meet. Repulsed because they were the self-identical.

Atrophy climaxes its tremulous cord down & down through yr anatomy founded by its throbbing banks, the river gluts by ramifying. A nexus we propose it always had to have been in this way, overdrawn through the understanding though thought, it's vegetating. Leaves pressed gold apart from shimmering, its essence struggled together in strife—green stipules we violate everywhere we graze.

But at night, We are convulsive engines, crunched all-over by pistons, the flowering recur, chronically stasis. You gesticulate into backwards congealing time displaced its sequence I'll be, when glaciers meltwater. You chunk thawed, I'm gagging after. Flesh through flesh through inverted plains the rotting vines scrawled yr names—enter the dust bowl. A punctuation marks the meeting place my body grows through its interval. Sand castles crashing, the trickle light fluxes out going, its sign, we waver. & unspool. The Pole stars unbound their fatalisms, mist ruddled the sound goes unremarked.

II. "They Didn't Touch Me."

In Hammond, Indiana, a woman holds the shape of gauze fluttering its power stations her between clotheslines, trailer-empty the creeks aren't safe here, anymore. Too many thumbs on the wrong hand, and wrist burns yr marred with looking like it; Time is justlike time. Polyphonic voices quicken a drawstrung world, she crashes in convolvulus, a heat ripens and settles it; that dew is an accident of sky.

Do you remember? What's revolving between yr body and its pit, the quarry drowned. anywhere noise is. Luminescent heads thickening memory water gelatinous, strike me from the record. I walked because I was called I don't remember whatfor.

In the morning my son will pick up the gun cartridge on the table, light deposits in an accounting somewhere fargone, I mean, I just know things now.

III. On the Radio

Brass is the metonymy of waking in the past, shedding petals, yr shuddering as the blood evacuates my face, my face engendered when you brushed it. Two lines in exit, and soot crosses. The leading lines of cartography, yr murmuring something I can't recover because I once did and scrabbling into my knees, trying to locate it, the embodied junction. Behind skin, it repeats its elision, falling asleep.

"I want to be closer" we tried

Nosediving, after it bottomsout. To rust

I'm Sorry It Didn't Come Out.

"There's a parenthesis for what's inside me. if you fillspace, it's an infinity symbol." I'm glowing with the alien hand prints fanning across my chest, patteddown from a fire. Who sets it, renews?

In Iowa I am always farming these ploughlines, an etude that rounds the meandering. Thought tractor beams clashed. These solvent notes, but grain seeds are unbreakable. Until they spill, profusely feathers.

Paint decays the red grain of a supporting wall I will remove it in the last act. First, I wake when dawn scintillates its fever. A flattening plane corresponds with it and do you understand yet? I was chosen.

Fox stink ruts in the clearing, the air fog forecasts clarity recedes. Into a prior arrangement, I insert the encased vessels, life proliferate. And the river chews its dreaming of us.

Like, Catfish will gnawthrough yr bones building an early frost orchestra, you armed it against us. A murky green the man is discovered inside the salt table. His body bloat transcends the desideratum of a profile. Then, a man in black comes and I take his pencil. "Everywhere," I say when he asks what they did to me.

My body? The Cattails caught dry reed stock. The enigma is foreclosed upon because the root toreout earth. I wait through the season of porches, and the ground dilated inside its yaw, a rocking chair rearights, loses it again. A plastic chair befalls a tornado, you tried to take its transcript down. This is theodicy. It figures endlessly, regurgitating into a silence that gestures. And I make leftovers from the case the broken embryos make. Squelching into a corner, ontological debris.

It takes months for the grass to transgress the circles you left me behind.

You Were Twilight Personified. Deepbruise

We're togetherbound by the field, the field is the neither side, I can see it because you're receding from view. I was just deepending my feelings, as a deer steps, the floodplains. The underneath of the world covers over:

Lability takenback to symbiosis

When I unlace my self from yr fingers, I screamcrash "I'M NOT SURE I CAN SING THIS, RIGHTNOW!"

You hand over the object drive this repression is a compromise.

We are obliterated by its phenomena and the ecstasy is a catalyzing of its release. You & I always, always stand out. In a field, the tornado is coming to recoup its dividend. So hold yr equipment at the bodily levels, hunch over and wind-slashed erosions, give in.

Footfall, god's grace, a rattling currency. And when he descends

he sings, "I am the solar flare that cut you up from the ground."
Impossible zeroes

I ever wish I knew. The choreography to this slow dance, earth
retrogrades to—

When we kissed, I briefly parted from a fire. In the south, a
furnace for the building blocks of nothing. Fallout

The Cesarean Scar

The cesarean scar grimacesmiles across her torso, bent by lightning bifurcations falling-striated down it. She duct tapes its mouth shut to fit herself in the shape of answer. But when she goes to undo the tape, it rips chunks out flesh from flesh from meat. Blood collects and in viscosity and with electrostatic force, the ley lines of the body divulged. A monumentally haunted cartographer draws their fingers through the gash time doesn't suture it's just repeating itself in tightening circles.

I know what it sounds like when she cries and when she gasps, as the tape splits, tugging the breath back through teeth. That music hissed, locating them. Jess'ca I wanted to be beautiful for

AppalachianNothing.

I continuously rewrite the section where I confront the Queen of Space, who is Kristeva:

I am running in gold cosmic body armor down through the hallways, aisles lapsing behind me like the other questions you forgot to posit in a right accounting of the space, the time it takes to arrive in the hesitation beneath her feet, do I exist? I ask the Queen of Space, over & over again, do I exist?

My mother is weeping on the floor, a deer collapsed into its soft hind legs, an accordion cataracting within its mythological song, it won't play, now. Her body is burbling foam, hiccups soughed, and hers is, is swept away.

Nietzsche says there is no unconditional relationship.

So The Involuntary Serial Killer smashes their fist through the radio receiver in my car, are they trying to get at the wires behind the face plate? If you could reach it would you die from the excess electricity? As the radio signature kisses yr finger tips in static communiques, a self revulsed, exposed wires fray, yr still sparks? I am trying to drive my car into the lake, and you are sitting here beseeching me with the one thought I don't care "if you die. I don't care."

doiexistdoiexistdoiexistdoiexistdoiexist

An immobilized semiological block I am also sobbing in the car behind it when people aren't looking for my body in the pastureside I left it in, do I

"Maybe, baby, maybe not—better not to think about it, rightnow" Kristeva, Queen of Space, tilts her chin up and & up and her lips press out an exit prayer in the center of my forehead.

Then, I break into my car.

S1 = **0** 0 0 0 0 0 0 0 0 0 ...

S2 = 1 **1** 1 1 1 1 1 1 1 1 ...

S3 = 0 1 **0** 1 0 1 0 1 0 1 0 ...

S4 = 1 0 1 **0** 1 0 1 0 1 0 1 ...

S5 = 1 1 0 1 **0** 1 1 0 1 0 1 ...

S6 = 0 0 1 1 0 **1** 1 0 1 1 0 ...

S7 = 1 0 0 0 1 0 **0** 0 1 0 0 ...

S8 = 0 0 1 1 0 0 1 **1** 0 0 1 ...

S9 = 1 1 0 0 1 1 0 0 **1** 1 0 ...

S10 = 1 1 0 1 1 1 0 0 1 **0** 1 ...

S11 = 1 1 0 1 0 1 0 0 1 **0** 1 ...

. . . .

. . . .

. . . .

S = 1 0 1 1 1 0 1 0 0 1 1 . . . And this gesture doesn't mean
anything, it's already gone.

He kicks her head so hard it leaves a dent I am

writing in dent deaddent she's worried about what it did to

her mind

Kicking concrete curb stop typography stop

cracks the paved flower clusters ambivalently aired

face tornup face fissures leaking time poring bore holesthrough
the compact snapped shut

what did I leave in there

All I know is it don't staydead

Playdead

AllTime Sadness Greats

And sadness is a radical I set it oscillating in space, it's just me shattered by the rhombus face of the past, I can never return from.

We should be vying for an opening, in the bar it dims you say it's scary starting to, get addicted to, anything and I know you've been following me here for a long fucking time.

"Isn't it weird how yr death instinct is the practical joke, he never played, a broken wrist. Flicking rocks. I mean, the mold just appears on the bodies, that's why. I love. This scene. Because we're learning nobody destroyed the world, the problem is that you receive it, in parts. Because we were only quasi-damned after all. Flashing instantaneously-nothing.

Tell me what you were looking for, when you died? A retro grade?

And Yr dislocated, a mannequin falling to the floor doubles

Yr inimitable nature, because the mirror necessitated the plummeting through. A haunting ersatz—yr in the rejection an image overturns.

The worst Janus mask has no reverse face. Do you? Need a hand or a guide. Just ask and supernumerary objects as-if appear—

I.

Yr mouth collapses into a tractor bream as tachyons filterback from the future past through the voices, singing in the dusky bar, smoke crags, and the melody repeats because the needle is broken can't find its groove, a coordinate system failing gravity. I lurch into the next drink and the next slumps me into my barstool—Slop. Messy fingers, these rivulets run them, reading hieroglyphs behind glass. When a time machine corrects an adjacent corner with the waxy castoff, figure of Mark Twain— he's not traveling though just dialing on the wrong telephone. In this immemorial bar when the hour's uncertain we raise the glass searching for the signal instead.

But I crop the picture looking for yr hands. As the needle slides between membranes of an eye lids closed. The pricking denotes us we were visionbound, seizing upon the city bound for unreal chains. But with one hand freedup I undo the latches around the topological map, and the skyscrapers release. Inkling ghosts, they could float up&up because they were behind a mist, unseasonably warm. Do you want this slow dance? There's time now because the music never stops. Will we get up?

"Do go somewhere."

II. The Worst Thing Is When You

Flinch-pulled away. So I drive 1,2,3,4 hours toward the river, a benediction you leave your face behind, the water rises because you came, begging for my mask will we ever find it? When cognition breaks, the illusion compromises. Itself. A hammer for the two eyes, were black holes. Nobody else. A fission succumbs there—

An automaton committing suicide, repetitively, you were love's captivation. And the crater bed fumes because we were buriedin inanimate nature: the illusion of the senses, each blade corresponds with its edge and I am trying to come to—one.

The basalt flows, pouring currents tangled. I make up my mind before I have the time to deliberate that a choice was occurring and the backwards work was thought. You are entropic vertices, nested in the meeting after points, it's a climax if you're looking up from down.

Anywhere the vacuum touched, slough yr skin, void as antimatter, I do renew it. But only over there

Will he ever catch an outgoing line?

A Song I'm Too Afraid to Listen to/ In the Powers of Horror, I release You!

In the sadgirl lost punk house downcast record store ephemeral debris, to the bottom of the sea-floors regurgitated in Providence, she is telling me how her grandparents used to hold hands and sing, "what ever will be, will be." In the forests, a teenage fairy, but you get beatup on trains, so keep yr wings poised and alarming. He came in from the hills, a throbbing world, where she practices playing brass instruments they attenuate the ache. He's her family now and they like taking the walk around the arbor, the clobbering westside factories, a memory is here and no place other. Then, the cops came and he dropped the canister, a broken meadowside. Years and years in purgatory, you can't vote for no descent—into the state. Drop acid in the woods, what was your name? I've lost something to these hills, declivities trace it back. Dissimilitude, He takes care of us.

I feel so gravity sick in the attic, but she is smiling. Baby, show me your front teeth.

Moving boxes between warehouses it's a waltz I'm so afraid of.
Dying without my things, my things. I'll toss them out, Here—

Sometimes deadstars just find eachother, don't you know. You
are always seen like this

Que sera

Blind walls, a force field, and sorry's I'm so. Sorry's

Who'll protect you, at night?

Hush.

The worst magic trick I learned as a child was how to identify a sorcerer who can, through their attentiveness, inaugurate your very being and, in the next instance, abolish it. Am I always seen like this?

Shaky face shoved into ashsmudged bedsheets, hulking my flexed body into a receding circle, without a connection, I sob and mumble "when no one is looking, I still—"

And I Perform This Act Without Scaffolding

In the vision I'm running on a track that's the edge of a circle so wide it looks straight unwinding and the abusive people are always just ahead of me, trackwired rabbits I can't see their faces we're running through a forest of impossibly tall self identical trees and there's no body else there except my parents on the sidelines cupping their mouths yelling "no one else is gonna want you and you can't do this alone yr broken Jessica baer you're so bustedup a sparking set of wires where yr heart should be" Beating, so I haul ass after Whomever, chasing phantasms while a quote in my head I can't place says the neurotic is afraid of a disaster occurring which has always-already happened in the past (immutable?) and I'm hallucinating music again until we arrive at exactly this part of the song rightnow where I collapse on my knees turning over gravel: dust and gasping turn to look at my parents and say "oh shit OH SHIT" I start crying because "that's how you feel about yourselves, that's why you stayed here" in the soliloquy section I confess that I was chasing you because you were trying to exit the world and I was scared you'd do it, too so I got stuck where a chorus rises like "jessica baer you can't resolve anybody you just love chaos or maybe you're a masochist or you dont know how to need yrrrself or..." I don't solve for x I stare blindly outside the positivistic smokescreen where things are ended by variables, a teleology. Yr varying powers of uncountable infinities.

I take violated people into my arms (after asking for consent to touch them) and say anything, it doesn't mean anything now but it's a memory burning, deadstars. And it does hurt and I'm sorry. I wrote these words to reach you before you go I wrote these words because we were always alone with that void lonely yr sownupwith because yr a person in my poems I could love this, sometime.

In every movement an exhausted prayer for grace & anti gravity but I keep finding myself in these uncannily familiar corners asking myself do you remember why we came here? And the truth is I wasn't going anywhere I was just running away because I didn't know what else could be made & still don't the universe is shimmering though which means Lucifer is crying while he eats human hearts, like always: I never stayed

*Addendum: Subducted Time

The auditory hallucination I've been experiencing since I left an abusive person in 2016 is my brain's attempt at a hyper-completion of ambient sounds it's a PTSD-related phenomenon in the complicatedly intertwining zone between the body and the mind where my dysregulated autonomic nervous system and my hypervigilance device eachother together to gather me away from

what is ruptured-time

and you're not here in the pause but the wreck in my body keeps gathering

the gestaltic debris of the past and superimposing it on the

leveled present so that i'm not here i'm not anywhere
at all where am I

and this *is* fucking frustrating

in the present tense

I am synthesizing into blades

fallback inside me

cutout

Epilogue: Reversing Time

Tonight N you will ask me what I think writing is? Lots of deliberative expressions will emerge, a profligate expenditure. But I think it's the binding of the heart and defibrillating it where

You watch the dog jump backwards into an anterior timeline, he reverses the animal sound of softpaws on the concrete, legible with holes. You are running through the tunnel ragged with raw feelings because it's the same source. An ambivalent little magnet in yr chest attuned to the electromagnetic field, the ground engendered the mystery of minerals, pocked marks and god is ground - penetrating radar.

What we feel is not ourselves? Entwine your fingers with mine and we'll plunge because there was no other direction on the map, my spirit is burning inside the headlights. Can I forgive my yrself for what I we saw these shadows hypervalenced.
And he's cutout and she's cutout and I'm

Just a scared animal—lead me on a leash. You don't have to go now, do you? It won't anneal, the jagged edge of absencing. It cuts you up

Is that why you were born? Or is it the way out

I say my prayer into the face of the lake, the weather man absconds the scene to derive the sizings of infinity a gesture time displaced. It reaches me once and never again

N I wanted to reunify with the lake in the tumultuous night that cries because it falls through the daylight-arches in extension. I thought it was scintillating with the onemind and I rescind all my other visions I won't live for other people I will have to be both and

It's tedious to try to remember why

Defection at the site of incision, beneath the breaching earth There, in the place of its absence:
A tomb to minerals, soft soliloquies the earth compacts

But a sleepwalking fetid figure continuously disrupts the narrative. He is riding his horse rapidly or softening into a canter across the terrestrial face, leaving footprints in the soot of a crater, floating its labyrinthine injunction the moon begins sucking apart.

I arrive at the counter level where machinic desire pneumatically reanimates the pistons driving toward my engined heart.

The bed of grass is dead the earth cups only its green memory. I take a hatchet and hackup its face.

Insectoid understanding writhes in the decay-eaten fissures as the body putresces continuing a chain reaction set off before the start.

Thought is malignant. Fait accompli you say referring to me because though we are seated Nick, we're the only ones dancing in this bar for deserters tonight.

I understand now I say meaning please touch me anywhere but here

Two eyes suddenly appear in the narrative and I raise them toward You and ask do you know when time changed hands? Maybe no one else is dancing because they haven't been asked. We are going away to the other side of history and I'm afraid that I've brought the wrong things did someone replace their things with my things

Who thought you into being?

I burrowed their voices strangling currents into knots. I write that There is a woman behind a glass door carrying a letter, and will you read it? There's time now. But I have forgotten my horse I have misplaced my hands. The glass door is not situated in the present narrative, which is why the anonymous rider continuously roves endlessly-aimlessly over the terrestrial plain.

That sucking sound is the void-anterior to language, I begin speaking to You across the distance in the gloamy candlelight, nuanced by the orange synthesizing shadows, your face is really there but the words fall a way toward the unnameable vortex instead, as the wind switches its way through the blank spots of the building interior.

And I am a thousand places fallendown.

Keep drinking until the light exhausts itself. Mea culpa I whisper into my exposed wrist bone, blood wrote. It will heal but only in the past.

The present is hemorrhaging and worse, we might—

Acknowledgements

"Midwestern Hypermnesia Surfaces," Tarpaulin Sky Book Award Shortlisted Finalist Excerpt (2019)

Thank you to the J. Allen Hynek Center for UFO Studies for allowing the use of the report form in the 'Abductions' section

Ulrich Jesse K. Baer received their MFA from Brown University in 2017. They were born in GA and grew up beneath southern power plants. They have a poetry chapbook with Magic Helicopter Press (*Holodeck One*, 2017), a science fiction chapbook with Essay Press (*At One End*, 2020), and have been included in journals such as Prelude Mag, Pinwheel, Bathhouse, Baest, The Tiny Mag, and Bone Bouquet. Today they love horses.